Dinosaurs

A Random House PICTUREBACK®

Dinosaurs
by Peter Zallinger

Random House New York

This title was originally catalogued by the Library of Congress as follows: Zallinger, Peter. Dinosaurs / by Peter Zallinger. New York: Random House, © 1977. [32]p.: col. ill.; 21 cm. (A Random House Pictureback) SUMMARY: Pictures and brief text introduce the characteristics of various dinosaurs. 1. Dinosauria—Juvenile literature. [1. Dinosaurs] I. Title. QE862.D5Z3 568'.19 76-24178 ISBN:0-394-83445-3 (B.C.); 0-394-83485-2 (trade); 0-394-93485-7 (lib. bdg.).

Millions of years ago dinosaurs roamed the earth. Some were small. Some were giant animals, different from any to be seen today. They weighed as much as five large elephants, and at least one kind of dinosaur grew to a length of almost 90 feet.

There were dinosaurs on earth for 120 million years, but all of them had disappeared long before the first humans lived. Yet we know how big they were, where they lived, and some of the things they ate. It is even possible to see dinosaur skeletons in museums today.

Most of what we know about dinosaurs has been discovered during the past 200 years. Scientists have been digging in many places around the world, searching for dinosaur bones.

When they find a dinosaur bone, they carefully remove it from rock and shale with special tools. Then they cover the bone with a coat of shellac. After that, the bone is wrapped in strips of burlap that have been dipped in plaster, and it is taken to a laboratory.

Trying to figure out how dinosaur bones fit together is a little like working on a jigsaw puzzle. Scientists also study the stone remains of dinosaur eggs, dinosaur footprints, and plants and insects that lived in the age of dinosaurs. All these

things are called *fossils*. Fossils formed when a dinosaur or other living thing made a print in the mud. After millions of years the mud turned to stone, and the print was left in the stone.

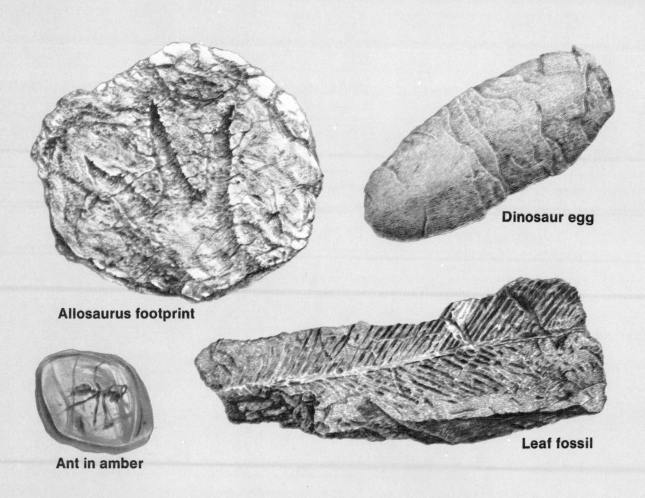

Dinosaur egg

Allosaurus footprint

Ant in amber

Leaf fossil

Hesperosuchus

Coelophysis

The ancestor of the dinosaur is the thecodont (THEEK-o-dont). There were many kinds of thecodonts. Hesperosuchus (hes-per-o-SOOK-us) is one example. This small hunter could probably run very fast on its strong hind legs, and may have used its smaller forelimbs for grasping its food.

The first true dinosaurs were the coelurosaurs (SEE-lur-o-sawrs). One of these—Coelophysis (see-LA-fuh-sis)— grew to a length of about eight feet and had a long, slender neck and tail. It also had long hind feet, and probably used its short front foot for hunting and eating.

As time passed, bigger dinosaurs began to appear. Some of these ate meat and others ate plants. Plateosaurus (plat-ee-o-SAWR-us) was mainly a plant-eater. Its front legs were long and sturdy, so scientists think Plateosaurus was able to walk on all four legs.

Plateosaurus

Teratosaurus (ter-at-o-sawr-us) was one of the early
meat-eating dinosaurs. Its head was much bigger than the head
of Plateosaurus. Teratosaurus had the strong jaws and sharp
teeth of a hunter. Its hind legs were long and powerful,
so Teratosaurus must have stood on two legs.

Teratosaurus

Ornitholestes (orn-ih-tho-LES-teez) was a small dinosaur that fed on winged reptiles such as Archaeopteryx (ar-kee-OP-ter-ix), as well as on lizards and small mammals.

Archaeopteryx had jaws, teeth, and a long bony tail like other reptiles. But it is the first known reptile with feathers.

Archaeopteryx

Ornitholestes

Stegosaurus (steg-o-SAWR-us) was a very different-looking dinosaur. Two rows of thin, sharp bony plates ran along its back, and there were four huge spikes at the end of its powerful tail. This new kind of plant-eater walked on all four legs.

Stegosaurus

One of the very largest dinosaurs was Brontosaurus (bron-toe-SAWR-us). This giant was about 70 feet long and probably weighed as much as 30 tons. Its long neck was good for reaching out for plants, but it had a tiny head and very small mouth. In order to feed its huge body, Brontosaurus must have eaten all day long.

Brontosaurus

Allosaurus (al-lo-SAWR-us) was less than half as long as Brontosaurus, but it could be a dangerous enemy to larger plant-eaters. It had the big head, strong jaws, and sharp teeth of a meat-eater. Its claws could rip through the tough hide of its prey.

Allosaurus

Camptosaurus (kamp-toe-SAWR-us) probably provided many a fine meal for the fierce Allosaurus. This plant-eater was only 7 to 18 feet long. Its long, flat skull was shaped differently from the heads of earlier dinosaurs. It could walk on either two feet or four.

Camptosaurus

The longest dinosaur that ever lived was Diplodocus
(dih-PLOD-uh-kuss). This plant-eater had a
very long tail and neck and a slender body. It
grew to be almost 90 feet long, about the
length of three school buses. Its head
was so small that scientists wonder how
Diplodocus managed to take in enough
food to keep alive.

Diplodocus

During the age of dinosaurs, even the seas were full of reptiles. Elasmosaurus (ee-laz-mo- SAWR-us) was 40 feet long, with strong paddlelike legs.

Its long neck and sharp teeth were good for catching fish. Ichthyosaurus (ICK-thee-uh- SAWR-us) looked like a fish but had no gills. Like other sea reptiles, it had to come to the surface of the water to breathe.

Elasmosaurus

Ichthyosaurus

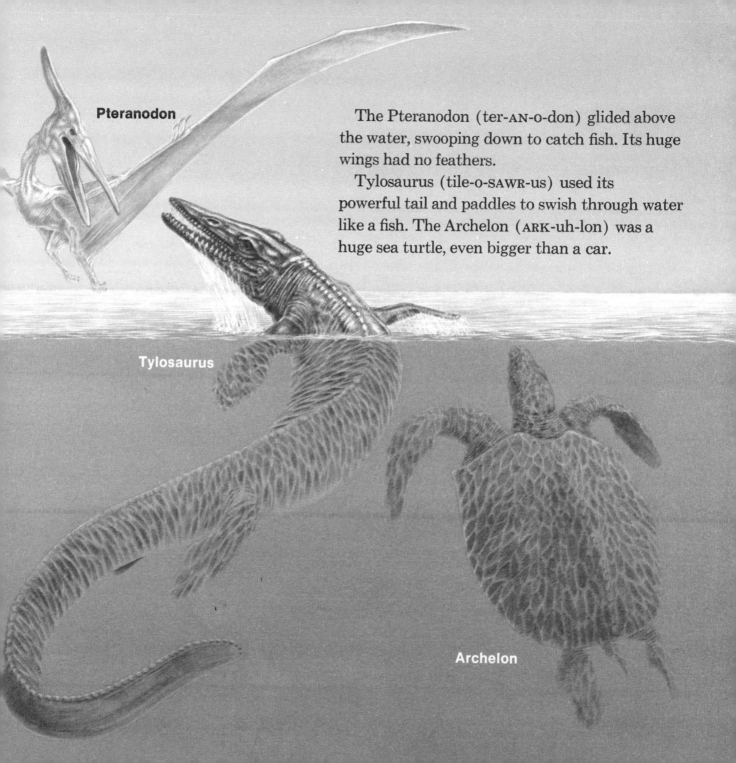

Pteranodon

The Pteranodon (ter-AN-o-don) glided above the water, swooping down to catch fish. Its huge wings had no feathers.

Tylosaurus (tile-o-SAWR-us) used its powerful tail and paddles to swish through water like a fish. The Archelon (ARK-uh-lon) was a huge sea turtle, even bigger than a car.

Tylosaurus

Archelon

As time passed, there were some plant-eaters that had horns. The Styraco-saurus (sty-rak-o-SAWR-us) was one of these. Six sharp spikes grew in a kind of frill around its neck, and a single sharp horn grew out of its nose.

Styracosaurus

The Monoclonius (mon-o-KLON-ee-us)
also had a large horn sticking out
of its nose, and two bony growths just
above its eyes. These horned dinosaurs
had good natural weapons to use against
their enemies.

Monoclonius

The duckbill dinosaurs were among the later types of dinosaurs. They were called duckbills because of their broad, flat front jaws.

Corythosaurus (kor-ith-o-SAWR-us) was a duckbill with a high, bony ridge on top of its head. This ridge must have looked like a helmet.

Another kind of duckbill, Lambeosaurus (lam-bee-o-SAWR-us), had a V-shaped bony crest on its head.

Lambeosaurus

Corythosaurus

Some duckbill dinosaurs grew
to be 40 feet long. The largest was
Anatosaurus (a-nat-o-SAWR-us).
Anatosaurus was a plant-eater,
like the other duckbills, and may
have had as many as 2,000 teeth.

Anatosaurus

Ankylosaurus (an-kile-o-SAWR-us) was one of the armored dinosaurs. Bony plates covered its back, and long spikes stuck out all around its low, thick body. Its clublike tail was tipped with a heavy mass of bone. Ankylosaurus was one plant-eater that probably did not have to worry about the fierce Tyrannosaurus (tie-ran-o-SAWR-us), king of the meat-eating monsters.

Ankylosaurus

Tyrannosaurus was 45 feet long and 20 feet tall. A six-foot man would not have reached to the knee of a giant eight-ton Tyrannosaurus. Tyrannosaurus depended on its huge head and massive jaws to grab and eat its prey.

Tyrannosaurus

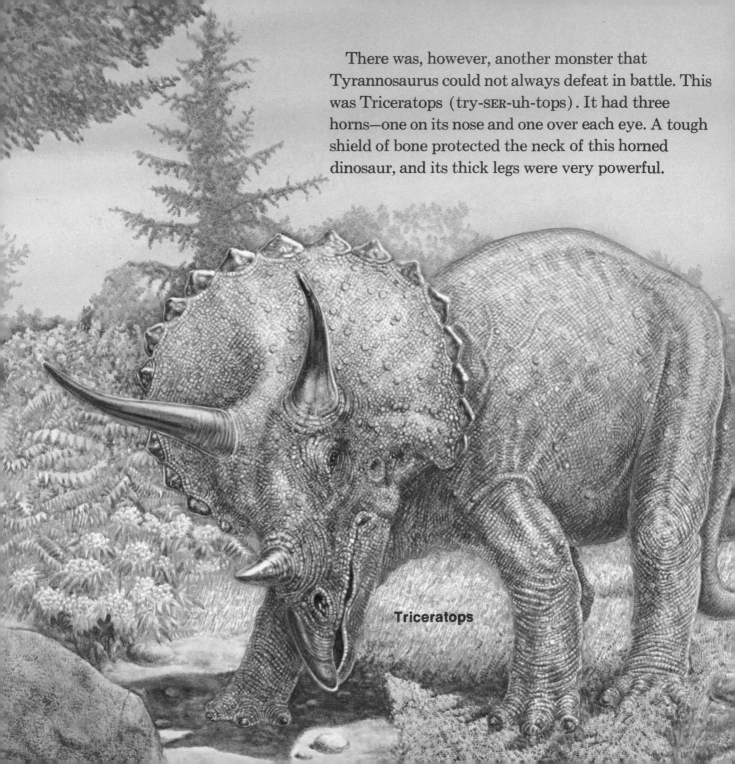

There was, however, another monster that Tyrannosaurus could not always defeat in battle. This was Triceratops (try-SER-uh-tops). It had three horns—one on its nose and one over each eye. A tough shield of bone protected the neck of this horned dinosaur, and its thick legs were very powerful.

Triceratops

Tyrannosaurus

The last of the dinosaurs died out about 70 million years ago. Scientists don't know why dinosaurs disappeared, and they may never know. Could their disappearance have been caused by a change of climate, by a change in food, or by some great world disaster? No one can be sure.

Whatever happened, it is important to keep in mind that dinosaurs lived on this earth for at least 120 million years. According to the most recent discoveries, humans have lived here for only a few million years.